The BIG RED TRACTOR

and the little village

Francis Chan

Illustrated by Matt Daniels

David C Cook

transforming lives together

THE BIG RED TRACTOR AND THE LITTLE VILLAGE
Published by David C Cook
4050 Lee Vance View
Colorado Springs, CO 80918 U.S.A.

David C Cook Distribution Canada
55 Woodslee Avenue, Paris, Ontario, Canada N3L 3E5

David C Cook U.K., Kingsway Communications
Eastbourne, East Sussex BN23 6NT, England

The graphic circle C logo is a registered trademark of David C Cook.

All rights reserved. Except for brief excerpts for review purposes,
no part of this book may be reproduced or used in any form
without written permission from the publisher.

The Web site addresses recommended throughout this book are offered as a resource to you.
These Web sites are not intended in any way to be or imply an endorsement on
the part of David C Cook, nor do we vouch for their content.

This story is a work of fiction. All characters and events are the product of the author's imagination.
Any resemblance to any person, living or dead, is coincidental.

Acts 1:8 quotation is taken from the New Century Version®. Copyright © 1987, 1988, 1991 by Word Publishing,
a division of Thomas Nelson, Inc. Used by permission. All rights reserved.

LCCN 2010927439
ISBN 978-0-7814-0419-8
eISBN 978-1-4347-0247-0

Text © 2010 Francis Chan
Illustrations © 2010 David C Cook
Published in association with the literary agency of
D.C. Jacobson & Associates LLC, an Author Management Company
www.dcjacobson.com

The Team: Don Pape, Kate Etue, Amy Kiechlin, Jack Campbell
Cover and Interior Illustrations: Matt Daniels

Manufactured in Shen Zhen, Guang Dong, P.R. China, in January 2014 by Printplus Limited.
First Edition 2010

4 5 6 7 8 9 10

012714

To my big brother Paul. Thanks for being an example of integrity. Sorry for beating you in every single sport while we were growing up.

Once upon a time,
in a happy little village,
a big red tractor lived in
a cozy little shed.

Each year when the snow started to melt, the villagers knew it was time to plow their field. So every morning they'd go out to the little shed and wake up the big red tractor.

They loved the powerful putt-putt, ka-boom noises he made. And they cheered because the big red tractor helped them with their hardest job: plowing the field.

Everyone worked together to move
the big red tractor through the field.
Half the villagers pushed him, and
the other half pulled him.

He smiled cheerfully, glad to help, even though they never seemed to move him very far.

The villagers worked very hard, and they always finished plowing the field just in time to plant delicious vegetables and sweet fruit before the rain came.

The rain fell from the sky
and watered the field.

Then the sun came out
and made the seeds grow.

Finally, the villagers gathered
all the food in large baskets.

Everyone celebrated. Everyone shared.
There was just enough food to feed the
whole village.

Then, one cold day, something amazing happened! Farmer Dave was cleaning out his attic and discovered a book tucked inside an old chest.

It explained how the big red tractor had been made, and it showed powerful things no one knew he could do.

Farmer Dave stayed up all night reading the book. He couldn't wait to tell everyone what he had discovered!

The next morning Farmer Dave gathered the villagers to tell them the good news: "The big red tractor can move on his own! If we fix him, he could plow the entire field in just one day!"

But nobody believed him. "There's no way that tractor can move on his own," they said. "It sounds like a fairy tale!" They laughed at him and went back to their work. This made Farmer Dave very sad.

But Farmer Dave didn't stop believing what he had read. Every night, while the villagers were asleep, Farmer Dave stayed up late fixing the big red tractor.

Finally, after many nights, Farmer Dave was done! He jumped onto the big red tractor and turned him on—putt putt, ka boom! He jumped in the driver's seat and had so much fun that he plowed the whole field that very night!

The next morning, the villagers woke up to a huge surprise! Their work was done for them! They would not have to spend many weeks pushing and pulling the big red tractor over fields of dirt.

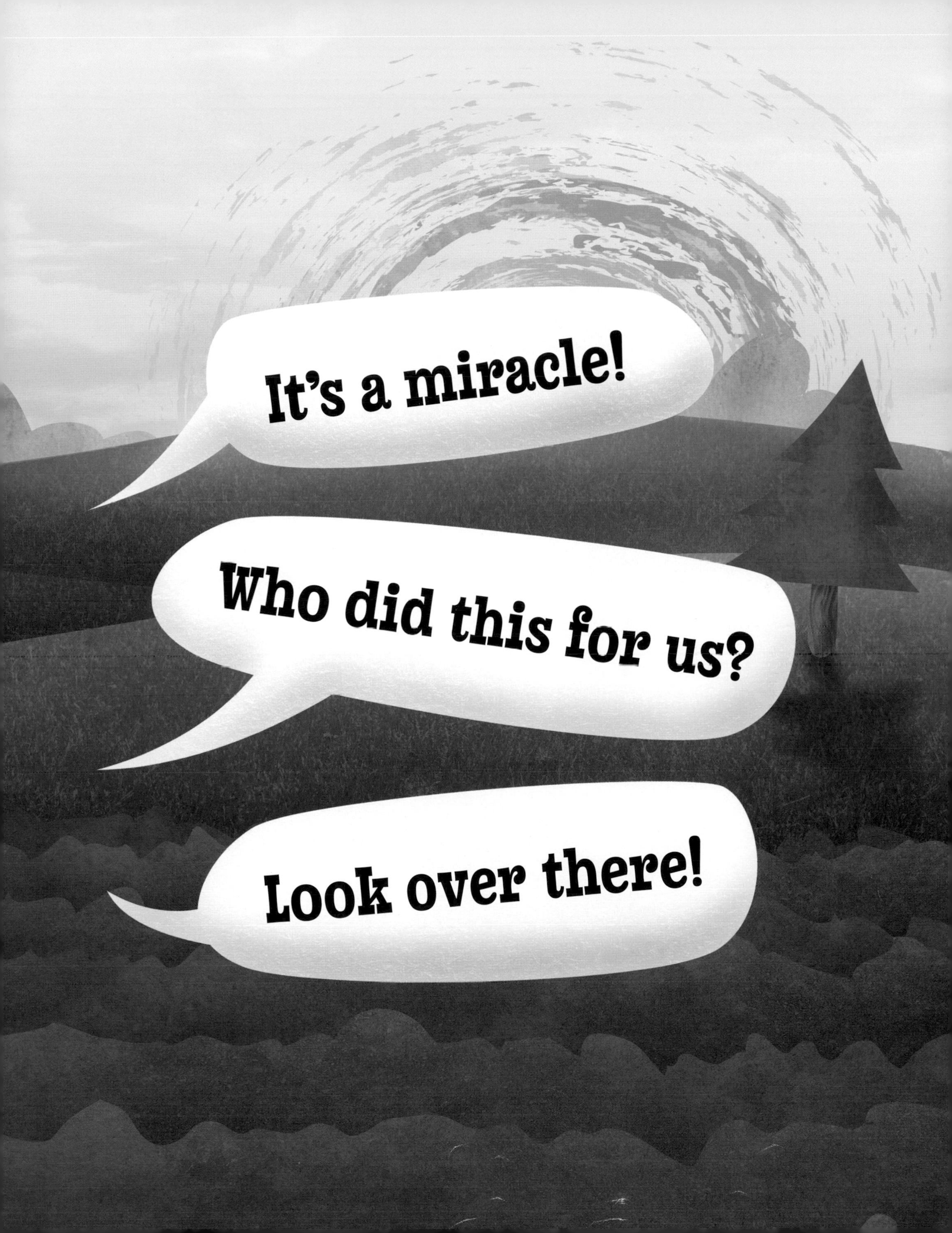
It's a miracle!
Who did this for us?
Look over there!

It was Farmer Dave sleeping on the big red tractor. The people shouted happily, "Farmer Dave was right! The tractor book is true!"

That year the villagers plowed and harvested many fields. They had so much extra food that they were able to share it with people in other villages who needed it.

When they visited other villages, Farmer Dave and the big red tractor always took the book with them so they could teach others the wonderful news they'd learned.

The little village kept sharing, and the villagers became known as the most generous people in the world.

Did you know that you are like the big red tractor? God made you, and He knows just how you work best.

He wrote a book full of truth that you can read to help you know how to live too.

The Bible tells us that if we try to do things on our own, we won't accomplish much. But if we trust in Jesus, God gives us His Spirit so we'll have new power: the power to love others and tell them about God.

God made us to be a blessing to others. Through the Spirit, we can do great things . . . just like Jesus!

When the Holy Spirit comes to you, you will receive power. (Acts 1:8)